# Captain's Log:
# SNOWBOUND

Erin Dionne

Illustrated by Jeffrey Ebbeler

Charlesbridge

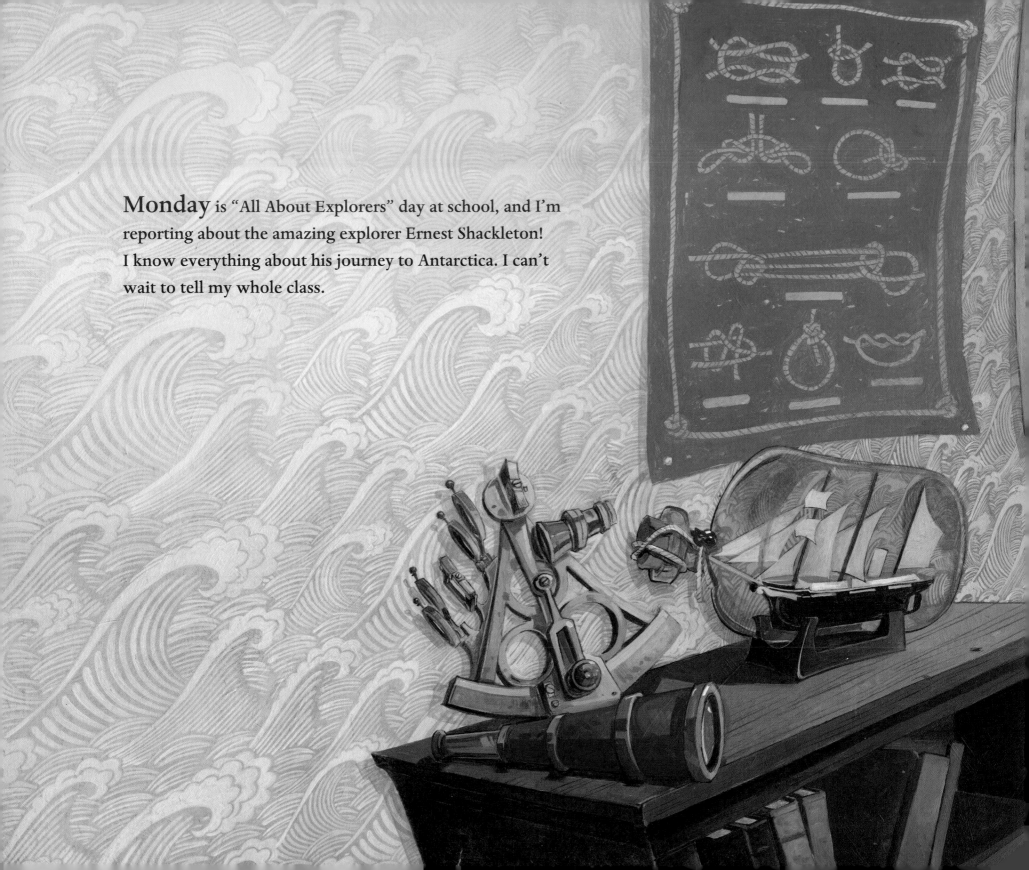

Monday is "All About Explorers" day at school, and I'm reporting about the amazing explorer Ernest Shackleton! I know everything about his journey to Antarctica. I can't wait to tell my whole class.

But there's a lot of snow falling outside right now. An *awful* lot....

CAPTAIN'S LOG.
DAY I. SNOWBOUND.

Our ship is stuck in ice and snow.
But we are prepared! Like Shackleton,
the first mate and I gathered provisions
and directed the crew to do the same. There's plenty
of hardtack, and everyone is cheerful—even the scallywag.

I shall record our adventure until our voyage resumes.

I remain, your faithful captain.

LATER. (DAY 1.)
The first mate and I led a shore party onto the glaciers. The wind howled! Snow flew! The crew cleared our skiff's path, and we explored. Shackleton recorded Antarctic seals and penguins, and we saw other creatures, too. Upon our return, we warmed ourselves with hardtack and conny onny.

Of note: My muffler is missing. Perhaps I left it behind?

Fur Seal →

Yeti?

muffler

Penguins →

CAPTAIN'S LOG. DAY 2. SNOWBOUND.

Neither the crew nor I expected this storm to last. The scallywag is trying our patience. He climbed halfway up the mainmast and sang a sea shanty before the crew retrieved him.

Also, I cannot locate my favorite tankard. I must command the first mate to keep watch over my belongings. . . .

Grog

tankard

LATER. (DAY 2.)

In all my days, I have never seen such a big storm! Everyone cleared ice and snow from the deck. Although it is unusual for a captain to perform such duties, I assisted. Shackleton himself pitched in and cared for each crew member on his ship, the *Endurance*.

Fie! My prized quill has disappeared from my desk. I am starting to wonder if the scallywag is responsible. . . .

Tomorrow we sail again. I hope.

quill

lifeboat

boiler    laboratory    pantry

fresh
water

Endurance

fresh
water?

pantry

boiler

laboratory

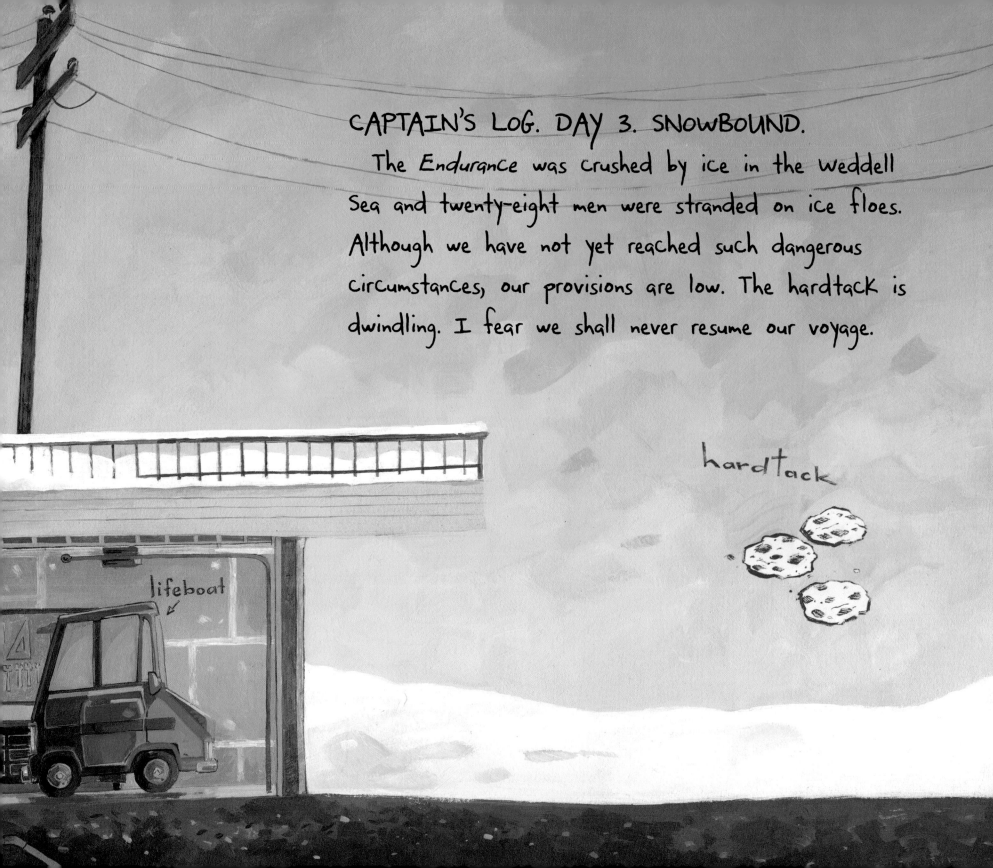

CAPTAIN'S LOG. DAY 3. SNOWBOUND.

The *Endurance* was crushed by ice in the Weddell Sea and twenty-eight men were stranded on ice floes. Although we have not yet reached such dangerous circumstances, our provisions are low. The hardtack is dwindling. I fear we shall never resume our voyage.

hardtack

lifeboat

LATER. (DAY 3.)

My map is gone! Could someone have used it for kindling? What scoundrel would do such a thing? I question the scallywag's loyalty.

Like Henry McNish, the carpenter on the *Endurance*, the scallywag may believe that he can lead the crew better than I can. I shall watch, and as Shackleton did with McNish, keep the scallywag close.

## UPDATE. (DAY 3.)

The scallywag has barricaded himself into his quarters with the remaining hardtack! All will be lost if the first mate and I don't act quickly.

My plan: Tonight I take back the hardtack and expose the ship's thief! If I do not return, fare thee well.

CAPTAIN'S LOG. DAY 4. SNOWBOUND.

Mutiny! The crew has turned against me. I am confined
to my quarters without the first mate for company.

Shackleton never felt such shame. His crew adored him
and followed his every lead.

My only joy is that the scallywag is also contained.

# Huzzah!

LATER. (DAY 4.)
I have been released and am at the helm again!
Scouts report that the storm has passed. We should
be able to resume our voyage on the morrow.

CAPTAIN'S LOG. DAY 5. DEPARTURE.

Anchors aweigh! The crew hoisted the sails, and our colors snapped proudly in the breeze. I called all aboard to the main deck. Even the scallywag cheered our return to the frosty sunshine and open sea.

I am prepared to share our story, and Shackleton's, in great detail. Like the great explorer before me, I await my next adventure.

## AUTHOR'S NOTE

Believe it or not, *Captain's Log: Snowbound* began as a series of Facebook posts. Between January 26, 2015, and February 17, 2015, approximately ninety-five inches of snow fell in the greater Boston area, where I live with my family. Ninety-five inches is one inch short of *eight feet*. My daughter's school was canceled for seven days in that time period. She'd go to school for one day, another snowstorm would happen, and then she'd be home for two or three days—then a weekend. My son was in preschool, and he basically never went. To laugh a little and keep sane, I started writing a captain's log on Facebook. The captain (me!) chronicled how we coped with our marooned state. Lots of other people, including my awesome editor, Karen Boss, were also stir-crazy from the storms, and my updates brightened their days. Spring finally came, and the posts became this book. Although I'm not a fan of snow and ice, I am pretty happy with how that record-setting winter turned out!

Shackleton's *Endurance* two months before she sank in the Weddell Sea on Oct. 27, 1915.
Credit: Library of Congress / Underwood & Underwood, ca.1916

## GLOSSARY

**conny onny:** tinned condensed milk, which sailors watered down to resemble fresh milk (before frozen milk was safe to bring on journeys)

**crew:** the people who sail or operate a ship or boat

**glaciers:** mountains of ice and snow

**hardtack:** a hard, crunchy biscuit that sailors packed as food

**helm:** the place from where the ship is steered

**muffler:** another term for scarf

**mutiny:** when part, or all, of the crew takes leadership away from the captain

**provisions:** food and other necessities packed on a ship

**quarters/quarter berth:** where a seaman sleeps

**quill:** a feather turned into a pen

**scallywag:** an undesirable character; a bad guy

**skiff:** a small boat

**tankard:** a large drinking cup, typically with a handle and hinged lid

"All About Explorers" Day Report: Ernest Shackleton
Born: February 15, 1874, County Kildare, Ireland
Died: January, 5, 1922, South Georgia Island
Occupations: merchant navy master mariner, journalist, explorer
Most Famous Goal: cross Antarctica over the South Pole
Ship's Name: the *Endurance*
Crew Size: 28 men, plus 69 sled dogs and 2 pigs

The story goes that Antarctic explorer Ernest Shackleton placed an advertisement for his third South Pole expedition in a London, England, newspaper that read: "Men wanted for hazardous journey. Low wages, bitter cold, long hours of complete darkness. Safe return doubtful. Honour and recognition in event of success." The ad is probably a myth, but however he found them, plenty of men wanted to go with him. He hired a captain and a crew of twenty-seven, and they set sail on the *Endurance* on August 8, 1914, from Plymouth, England. Shackleton met up with the ship in October, and they departed from South Georgia Island—the last island before Antarctica—on December 5, 1914.

In January 1915, the *Endurance* became trapped in ice in the Weddell Sea, near Antarctica. Shackleton's men lived on the boat and ice for months. They nicknamed the stuck ship "the winter Ritz," like a fancy hotel, complete with ship cat, Mrs. Chippy.

Shackleton led his men bravely, but one often disagreed with him. It is rumored that carpenter Henry "Chippy" McNish became impatient with Shackleton's choices. But McNish is considered a hero because he fitted the small skiffs for the journey to seek rescue, built the crew's sleeping quarters, and showed "grit and spirit," according to Shackleton.

On October 27, 1915, the frozen sea's pressure finally cracked the *Endurance*. Shackleton ordered the crew to abandon the ship. The crew now lived on ice floes—giant floating ice blocks. To keep their spirits up, the men played football and hockey and raced sled dogs.

Finally, in April 1916, the men squeezed into three skiffs and navigated across the Weddell Sea to Elephant Island. Shackleton set up camp, and then chose five men to continue sailing 800 nautical miles to South Georgia Island. Then they walked for thirty-six hours to a whaling station. The entire crew was rescued August 30, 1916.

Shackleton and his twenty-seven men spent 497 days without touching dry land and 752 days away from home. And every one of them survived.

To find out more about Shackleton and his expedition on the *Endurance*, use your favorite internet browser and search for "Shackleton Endurance." Be sure to look at the PBS *NOVA* website for lots of cool information, including an interview with Shackleton's granddaughter.

I read a bunch of books about Shackleton's expedition while researching this story, and my favorite was *The Endurance: Shackleton's Legendary Antarctic Expedition* by Caroline Alexander (Knopf, 1998).—E. D.

For my favorite scallywags, CP and HF—E. D.

For Isabel and Olivia—J. E.

Published by Charlesbridge
85 Main Street
Watertown, MA 02472
(617) 926-0329
www.charlesbridge.com

**Library of Congress Cataloging-in-Publication Data**
Names: Dionne, Erin, 1975– author. | Ebbeler, Jeffrey, illustrator.
Title: Captain's log: snowbound / Erin Dionne; illustrated by Jeffrey Ebbeler
Description: Watertown, MA : Charlesbridge, [2018] | Summary: Excited to give his report on
    explorer Ernest Shackleton in school, and frustrated by a monstrous snowstorm that has left
    his family and city snowbound, a boy imagines himself on a voyage where he and his crew
    (his family) are trapped by the ice, just like his favorite explorer and the ship, Endurance.
Identifiers: LCCN 2017028985 (print) | LCCN 2017057142 (ebook) | ISBN 9781632896834 (ebook) |
    ISBN 9781632896841 (ebook pdf) | ISBN 9781580898256 (reinforced for library use)
Subjects: LCSH: Shackleton, Ernest Henry, Sir, 1874–1922—Juvenile fiction. | Blizzards—Juvenile fiction.
    | Imagination—Juvenile fiction. | CYAC: Shackleton, Ernest Henry, Sir, 1874–1922—Fiction.
    | Blizzards—Fiction. | Imagination—Fiction.
Classification: LCC PZ7.D6216 (ebook) | LCC PZ7.D6216 Cap 2018 (print) | DDC [E]—dc23
LC record available at https://lccn.loc.gov/2017028985

Printed in China
(hc) 10 9 8 7 6 5 4 3 2 1

Illustrations done on Fabriano Artistico hot-press watercolor paper,
    then combined with ink drawings in Photoshop
Display type set in Celestia Antiqua by Mark van Bronkhorst
Text type set in Dante MT by The Monotype Corporation and FG Deanna's Hand by Deanna L. Deaton
Color separations by Colourscan Print Co Pte Ltd, Singapore
Printed by 1010 Printing International Limited in Huizhou, Guangdong, China
Production supervision by Brian G. Walker
Designed by Martha MacLeod Sikkema